My Sister Has a New Computer

by David Parker
Illustrated by Margeaux Lucas

Scholastic Inc.
New York   Toronto   London   Auckland   Sydney
Mexico City   New Delhi   Hong Kong   Buenos Aires

To my cousins, Richard and Ronald.
— D.P.

For my "sister" Marina, for all those great emails, besos.
— M.L.

ISBN-13:978-0-439-87123-5
ISBN-10:0-439-87123-9

12 11 10 9 8 7 6 5 4 3 2 1   7 8 9 10 11 12/0

Printed in the U.S.A.
First printing, January 2007

Chapter One
The New Computer

My sister, Stacy, has a new computer.
It came in a huge box this morning.
The box had little tiny popcorns in it.

"This is my computer," says Stacy.
"But you can have the box."
I like to play with the tiny popcorns.
I like to make houses out of huge boxes.
But I like Stacy's computer better than boxes or popcorn.

The computer has a little mouse and
a big screen.
It has a keyboard that clickety-clacks.
The screen is full of bright colors.
Stacy's computer beeps and whirs
and plays music.
"I love my computer," Stacy says.
"I love your computer, too," I say.

"Can I push one of the buttons?" I ask.
"No," Stacy says.
"Can I hold the little mouse?" I ask.
"Not today," Dad says.
"Can I make it play music?" I ask.
"Maybe when you're older," Mom says.

I wish I had a computer.
So I make one in my room.
I use the empty box for the screen.
I use Fluffy's stuffed mouse.
I use the TV remote control for the
keyboard.

"What is that?" asks Stacy.
"It's my computer," I say.
"Clean up this mess," says Mom.
Even Fluffy does not like my
computer.
She takes her mouse away.

Chapter Two
Do Not Touch

Stacy puts a sign on her door.
It says, NO LITTLE BROTHERS ALLOWED.
"But I'm not little," I say.
No one listens.

"Do not touch the computer,"
says Mom.
"Do not play with the computer,"
says Dad.
"Do not touch anything in my room,"
says Stacy.

"I promise not to touch the computer,"
I tell Mom.
"I promise not to play with it,"
I tell Dad.
"I promise not to touch anything in
your room," I tell Stacy.
"Good," they say.

Stacy spends a lot of time with
her computer.
"Do you want to play outside?" I ask.
"No," she says.

"Do you want to read a book with me?" I ask.
"Not today," she says.

"Do you want to ride bikes?" I ask.
"Maybe tomorrow," she says.

"Can I play with your computer?"
I ask.
"Maybe when you're older," she says.

I stare at the computer for a very, very long time.
I wish very, very hard for my own computer.
But I will not touch Stacy's computer.
I will not break my promise.

Chapter Three
What Do I Do Now?

Mom is taking Stacy to her piano lesson.
"We will play outside when I get home," Stacy says.
"Okay," I say. "Will you read a book with me, too?"
"Sure," she says. "We can ride bikes, too. No computer today."
I smile.
She smiles, too.

Stacy and Mom leave.
Stacy's bedroom door is open.
She took down her NO LITTLE BROTHERS
ALLOWED sign.
That makes me happy because I am
not little.

Oops! She left her computer on.
I go into her room.
I walk up to the computer.

It beeps and whirs and plays music.
The screen is full of bright colors.
The little mouse looks lonely.
I could play with the mouse.
I could make the keyboard
clickety-clack.

But I promised not to touch it.
It belongs to Stacy.
It does not belong to me.

We will play outside when Stacy
gets home.
We will read a book.
We will ride bikes.

But right now, Stacy is not here.
I have to wait a long time to play
outside, and read a book, and
ride bikes.
The computer is here right now.

What should I do?
What would *you* do?